KT-116-109

CONTENTS

FACTS ABOUT SOMALIA

- Somali people come from many different clans.
- Many Somalis are nomadic. That means they travel from place to place. They search for water, food and land for their animals.
- Somalia is mostly desert. It doesn't often rain there.
- The camel is an important animal to Somali people. Camels can survive for a long time without food or water.
- Around ninety-nine per cent of all Somalis are Muslim.

SOMALI TERMS

ayeyo (ah-YEH-yoh) grandmother

baba (BAH-baah) a common word for father

halwa (HAL-u-wah) a sweet, chewy treat

hooyo (HOY-yoh) mother

jar (JHRR) a board game involving strategy

qalbi (KUHL-bee) my heart

salaam (sa-LAHM) a short form of Arabic greeting, used by many Muslims. It also means "peace".

wiilkeyga (wil-KAY-gaah) my son

CHAPTER 1

FESTIVAL SCHOOL TRIP

"Please line up, everyone!" called
Ms Battersby. She was standing next to
the school bus with a clipboard.

Children rushed towards the bus.
It was a bright Friday morning, and
Sadiq's class was going on a school trip
to a multicultural festival!

Sadiq, Manny and Zaza had just
arrived at school.

"I am really excited about the Festival of Nations," said Sadiq. "*Hooyo* says it's a big event."

"I'm excited to try all the different foods they'll have!" said Zaza with a grin. He loved food of every kind, and he couldn't wait to sample it all.

"We'd better hurry up if we don't want to miss the whole thing!" said Manny. The three boys raced over to get on the bus.

"Good morning, Ms Battersby!" they called out together.

"Good morning, boys," she replied and looked down at her clipboard. "I think you three are the last ones here. Hop on!"

"Whew! Just in time!" said Sadiq.

The boys boarded the bus and gave their classmates fist bumps as they walked down the aisle looking for seats. The students chatted excitedly together as the bus travelled to the huge exhibition centre. Food, music, games, crafts – there would be so much to do at the festival!

As they pulled into the exhibition centre car park, Ms Battersby stood up. Announcement time.

"You will have a couple of hours to walk around and check out the stalls," she said. "If you brought money and your parents said it was okay, you can buy small souvenirs."

"What time should we come back?" asked Manny.

"I will expect everyone to meet here by the bus at one p.m. sharp," said Ms Battersby. "And remember to stay with a buddy!"

The children clambered off the bus and hurried towards the festival.

"Wow!" said Zaza to Manny and Sadiq. "Where do we start?"

They stared at the exhibition floor. It was a huge area with high ceilings and rows of stalls and tables and stages that seemed to go on forever. They could hear music and chatter, smell delicious foods and see flags and colourful banners everywhere they looked.

"I suppose we should start at the front!" suggested Manny. "We'll work our way from front to back to make sure we don't miss anything."

"Oh COOL!! Drums from Cuba!" said Sadiq, pointing to a nearby stall. "Look at all the different sizes!"

"Do you think they'll let you try one?" asked Zaza. "Ask the man at the stall."

Sadiq walked shyly up to the man. "Hi, I'm Sadiq," he said. "Could I please look at one of your drums?"

"Nice to meet you, young man!" said the older gentleman, smiling. He had a white beard and a bald head. "My name is Mr Ruiz. Why don't you try this one? It's small enough to hold with one arm and play with the other."

Sadiq's eyes widened. He took the drum and tried some beats on it.

Bam-ba-dum-da dum-dum boom!

"That's pretty good," said Mr Ruiz, smiling. "You've done this before."

"I really like playing musical instruments," said Sadiq.

"You're welcome to stop by again if you like," said Mr Ruiz. "I'll be here all day."

Sadiq shook the man's hand and thanked him.

"Did you hear that?" Sadiq asked his friends excitedly. "Mr Ruiz thinks I am pretty good!"

"Yeah, we heard it," said Manny, smiling. He gave Sadiq a playful shove.

"I think that stall is selling rugs," said Zaza. "What flag is that?"

"I think it's Pakistan, but I'm not sure," said Sadiq. He tilted his head, trying to remember. He and Nuurali had a big book of flags at home.

"You're right, it is Pakistan," said Ms Battersby. She had suddenly appeared behind the boys. "I love beautiful rugs, so I think I will join you here."

"These are really pretty, Ms Battersby," said Manny. "Are you going to buy one?"

"Maybe – if the price is right!" she said, winking. She walked ahead to talk to the woman running the stall.

The boys moved on. They found Vikram and Owen looking at small, carved statues at a nearby stall.

"What's up, guys?" asked Zaza. "What are those?"

"These are soapstone carvings," said Owen. He held up a small elephant with a design carved into its side.

"They're from Kenya!" added Vikram. "This is Mr Kinuthia. He's been telling us how he makes them."

"Oh, cool!" said Sadiq. "How much is one piece, Mr Kinuthia? I think my mum would like one."

"For you, only ten dollars," said Mr Kinuthia. "How about this one? It's a baby giraffe."

"Oh, thanks, Mr Kinuthia!" said Sadiq. "My hooyo is going to love it!"

***

Throughout the morning, the kids explored all there was to do at the festival.

They listened to some men performing a type of music called throat singing, which was very deep and loud!

They tried weaving grasses at a stall where women were making beautiful baskets.

And Zaza tried *lots* of sweet treats. But then he had to stop because his stomach began to hurt.

Sadiq looked at his watch, a gift from **Baba**. "Guys, it's time to head back," he said.

Manny offered Zaza the last bit of his mango smoothie, but Zaza shook his head and rubbed his stomach.

Manny patted his friend's shoulder and threw his cup into a recycling bin. Then they headed for the bus.

As the students took their seats, Ms Battersby ticked off their names on her clipboard.

"We had so much fun, Ms Battersby," said Zaza. He waved a tiny Somali flag he'd bought.

"Yeah, it was great!" Odin said and waved a flag for Norway that he had purchased.

Seeing his friends' flags gave Sadiq an idea. "Do you think we could have our own festival, Ms Battersby?" he asked. "We could all have stalls with things from different countries."

Aadya said, "Ooh, let's!"

Suaad clapped her hands excitedly. Other students nodded eagerly too.

Ms Battersby tapped her chin in thought. "That sounds like a great idea, Sadiq," she said. "I'll talk to Mr Kim. I think he'd love to help us host our own multicultural festival."

The kids all cheered as the bus rumbled back to school.

CHAPTER 2

LOTS OF LADDU

"Hi, Vikram!" said Sadiq as his friend opened the door on Saturday morning. Vikram had invited Sadiq and Owen over to play basketball.

"Hi, Sadiq!" replied Vikram. "Come on in!"

"Mmm, what smells so good?" asked Sadiq, sniffing the air. "Is your nani baking? She must have known I was coming!"

"Good guess!" said Vikram, laughing. "She's making laddu in the kitchen. I am sure she'll give you some. She likes you because you always compliment her cooking!"

"Hello, Nani!" said Sadiq as they went into the kitchen. "Vikram said you're making laddu. Smells good!"

"Hello, beta," said Nani, smiling. "I thought you'd like these. They're cooling now but you can have them later."

"Thank you so much, Nani," said Sadiq, hugging her. "I can't wait!"

"Hey, Owen, Sadiq's here! Let's go and play!" Vikram called out to Owen, who was sitting in the living room rolling a basketball under his feet.

"Coming!" said Owen. The boys went into the garden, where Vikram's dad had set up a basketball half-court.

"What's the limit for how many laddu I'm allowed to eat, Vikram?" Sadiq teased.

"One day you're going to turn into laddu, Sadiq," joked Vikram.

"Okay with me!" replied Sadiq. "It reminds me of my favourite Somali dessert, called *halwa*."

"Oh, we have halwa too!" said Vikram. "Nani also makes that."

"What's halwa?" asked Owen, crinkling his nose. "It sounds weird."

"Oh, you'd really like it," said Sadiq. "It's sweet and chewy, a little like jelly.

I like to have it with milk."

"Me too!" said Vikram. "Nani always gives me a glass of warm milk with it."

"What's your favourite dessert, Owen?" asked Sadiq.

Owen looked thoughtful for a moment and then shrugged. "I can't think of any right now," said Owen. "I guess I like chocolate chip cookies."

"Those are definitely one of my favourites too," said Vikram. "Extra gooey is the best!"

"*Melty* and gooey!" said Sadiq in agreement. "Also great with a glass of milk!"

The boys played basketball until

Vikram's nani called out to them.

"Vikram! Sadiq! Owen!" she said.
"The laddu is cool and ready to eat!"

"Me first!" shouted Sadiq. They all
raced back inside the house.

***

Sadiq and Owen were walking back
home together. They lived down the
street from each other, just a few streets
away from Vikram.

"I am super-duper excited about our
festival of cultures!" said Sadiq. "I think
I might bring some halwa. I'll ask
Hooyo about some crafts."

"That sounds cool," said Owen
quietly.

Owen shuffled his feet and looked

down as he walked.

"I also have some Somali toys I could display. Oh, and a flag!" Sadiq was thinking of all the things he wanted to include at his stall. He was so excited that it took him a minute to realize Owen wasn't saying anything.

"What's wrong, Owen?" asked Sadiq, frowning. "Aren't you excited about the festival?"

"I want to be excited," said Owen with a sigh. "I just don't know what I can bring. I don't know that much about where we're from. Or even really where my family is from."

"Maybe you could talk to your mum and dad about it?" suggested

Sadiq. "I am sure they could help."

"I suppose I can ask," said Owen, looking down again. "But I don't think we have any special recipes or stuff like that from our culture."

"Don't worry about it," said Sadiq cheerfully. "I am sure there will be plenty of fun and food and all sorts of games! There will be something for everyone."

"Yeah, okay," said Owen. He didn't seem convinced by what Sadiq was saying, but he smiled at his friend anyway.

CHAPTER 3

MAKING PLANS

The next Wednesday, many kids gathered in the library after school. Mr Kim had volunteered to be the group advisor for the festival of cultures.

"Thank you for helping us out, Mr Kim!" said Sadiq. He was excited to see that so many students had shown up to help!

"You're welcome, Sadiq," said Mr Kim. "I love your idea of celebrating different cultures."

The group made plans to host different stalls that would each feature things from different cultures. They would share and show items to help teach others about their cultures, including food, games, clothing, toys, music, maps, flags . . . the ideas were endless!

"Zaza and Manny, how would you like to share a stall with me?" asked Sadiq, turning to his friends. "Our families are all from East African countries. We could all do something together!"

"Yeah, we're all from the Horn of Africa!" Manny pointed out.

"That's right!" said Zaza. "That can be the theme of our stall!"

"Suliat, do you want to do a West African stall with me?" asked Aadya. "Suaad is from East Africa, but she wants to join my stall."

"Yes, sounds fun!" said Suliat eagerly. "I wasn't sure how to do it by myself, so I'd be glad to work together."

"I can't wait to learn some cool stuff about West Africa," said Suaad, clapping.

"I think our countries might have a lot in common!" replied Aadya.

"I am doing a Cuban and Irish stall, as I have relatives from both countries," said Carter. "Anyone else want to join me?"

"I'll join you, Carter," said Auggie. "I'm part-Cuban!"

"And I'm part-Irish!" said Spencer. "I'll join you too!"

"Great!" said Carter. "I can't wait for you to try my mum's Irish potato farls!"

Soon all the kids were going off in groups of twos and threes. They worked at different tables to plan their stalls and to make flyers advertising the festival to friends and family.

Mr Kim noticed Owen sitting alone at the back of the room and walked over to him.

"Hi, Owen," he said, smiling kindly. "Is everything alright?"

Owen nodded. "Yeah, I just wanted to hang out here for a bit."

"Would you like to host a stall at the festival? Or join one of the others and help with their stall?"

"Um . . . I think I'll just stay here, if that's okay," said Owen, shaking his head.

Mr Kim nodded and smiled. "Well, let me know if you change your mind," he said. "The more people we have to help, the better our festival will be!"

Sadiq, Zaza and Manny were busy coming up with ideas for their stall.

"We should bring laddu and halwa," Sadiq said to his friends. "I can ask my mum to get some halwa from the Somali shop."

Vikram was at a table with Salma and Safwan, planning a stall about Indian and South Asian culture.

"Vikram, do you think your nani will make some laddu?" Sadiq leaned over to ask him.

"I bet she will," said Vikram, grinning. "I'll just tell her that you refuse to go to school if you don't get any."

"Don't get me in trouble!" said

Sadiq. He playfully threw a crumpled sheet of paper at his friend.

Mr Kim drew a large square on the whiteboard and then drew smaller squares inside it in a grid pattern.

"Once you know what cultural theme your stall will have, you can come and write it in one of these squares," he said. "Include names of the students who will be hosting the stall."

One student from each table went to pick a square on the grid. Soon the grid was filled with names of countries and regions: India, Ireland, Cuba, Norway, West Africa, East Africa, Mexico and more!

When it was time to go, Sadiq looked around for Owen. He was hoping they could walk home together.

"Where's Owen?" Sadiq asked Vikram.

"I don't know," said Vikram, shrugging. "I think he left. Maybe his mum picked him up already."

"Yeah, maybe," said Sadiq, thoughtfully chewing his lip.

CHAPTER 4

EXCITEMENT AND A WORRY

Later that evening, Sadiq was having dinner with his family.

"You need to stop bouncing in your chair, Sadiq," said Hooyo. "You might fall off."

"I am sorry, Hooyo. I'll stop," said Sadiq. "I am just so excited about the festival at school."

"Have you decided what you'll show at your stall, Sadiq?" asked Baba as he helped cut Amina's food.

"Well, I am definitely hoping to take halwa," said Sadiq. "I mean, if you're able to buy some halwa, Hooyo?"

"Yes, I can do that for you, *qalbi*," said Hooyo. "What else will you have? Maybe some crafts?"

"Yes! I thought maybe we could get some cowrie shells?" suggested Sadiq. "Visitors to our stall can string them into necklaces or bracelets."

"That's a great idea, Sadiq. I will see if they have them at the market," said Hooyo.

"Vikram asked his dad if he can

bring their pachisi game to his stall," said Sadiq. "He promised to be careful with it."

"Well, if you make the same promise to me, you can borrow my *jar* board to display," Baba offered.

"That's fantastic, Baba!" said Sadiq, jumping up to hug his dad. "Thank you! I will be very careful with it!"

Jar was a Somali board game that Baba was teaching Sadiq to play. Even though it was difficult to learn, Sadiq loved spending time with Baba as they played together.

"I can help with your stall, Sadiq," said Aliya. "What else do you need?"

"Everything!" said Sadiq, excited

to have his family's help with his project. He really wanted to show his classmates as much as he could about his family's Somali culture.

"I'll help too," said Nuurali. "I volunteer to sample all food before you take it to school."

"Ha! You're so funny," said Sadiq. But he knew his brother was just joking, so he didn't mind.

"Sounds like you'd better get started," said Hooyo, standing up. "You have a lot of work to do!"

Sadiq was just about to run over to the hall cupboard to find Baba's jar board when he remembered something.

"The first thing I need to do is check on Owen," said Sadiq. "He was so quiet at our festival meeting, and not excited at all."

"Was he unwell?" asked Baba. "Maybe it was just a long day and he was tired."

"No, I don't think that's it," said Sadiq, shaking his head. "I think something was bothering him about the festival."

"Maybe he doesn't know what to show at his stall?" suggested Nuurali. "Or he can't decide which group to join."

"Mr Kim said he could pick whichever he liked," said Sadiq.

"But Owen didn't want to. Then he left without saying goodbye."

Hooyo refilled her water glass from the pitcher. "Maybe he doesn't feel like he belongs to any of the groups," she suggested. "Every family is unique and has special traditions. But not everyone knows where their traditions come from."

"That's right, Sadiq," said Baba, nodding. "Some people have lived in this country a short time and have lots of traditions from their home countries. Other people have lived here a very long time and may not have a strong connection to a place. But any tradition that celebrates family and togetherness is a beautiful thing."

Sadiq thought about what Baba and Hooyo were saying.

"May I be excused?" he asked. "I have an idea and want to call Owen."

CHAPTER 5

FESTIVAL FUN FOR ALL

Finally, it was festival day!

Sadiq and all his friends and classmates had had a busy week. Their families had been helping them get ready, but it had still been a lot of work!

There was cooking, baking, knitting, painting and many other things the students and their families had done to get ready. Now, the day was finally here.

As Sadiq and his family arrived, they could see people streaming into the gym hall, carrying boxes and coolers full of treasures.

"Looks like it's going to be a great festival, qalbi!" said Baba. "I see quite a number of different flags."

"Some stalls have already been set up," said Aliya as they walked in.

"Why don't you help us unload and get everything set up, Sadiq," said Hooyo. "Then you can go and find your friends."

Sadiq hugged her. "Thank you for helping, Hooyo!"

They made their way over to the East Africa stall.

Manny and Zaza were just
beginning to unload their things.

"*Salaam*!" Hooyo said.

"Salaam!" they replied.

They busied themselves setting up
trays of halwa, the jar board and many
more items from Somalia, Ethiopia
and Kenya.

Hooyo helped Sadiq's little sisters,
Amina and Rania, set up some small
Somali craft items. They had brought
cowrie shells, beaded key chains, hijabs
and woven table mats to sell at the
stall.

When everything was ready, Sadiq
went to check on his other friends. As
he went, he could see signs everywhere.

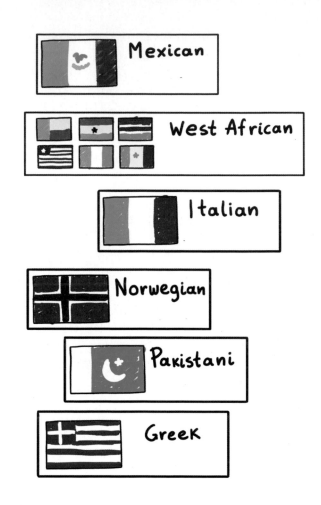

Sadiq spotted Carter and waved to him. Carter waved back and pointed up proudly at his *Cuban/Irish* banner.

Then he saw Vikram at the *South Asian* stall. "Save me some laddu!" Sadiq called out to him. Vikram gave him a thumbs-up in return.

Finally, Sadiq found the stall he was looking for. "Hi Owen!" he said as he approached the stall. "How's it going?"

"Really good," said Owen, grinning. He looked a lot more excited than he had before.

"Cool stall!" said Sadiq. He looked at the sign hanging above Owen:

Everywhere!

"Thanks for your idea, Sadiq!" said Owen. "I'm relieved that I didn't have to choose one culture or tradition."

Sadiq smiled. "It looks great! I bet a

lot of people are going to like it,"
he said.

A few other kids had joined Owen
in helping plan the stall when they
heard about the idea. They had filled
their stall with big bowls of popcorn,
flags from lots of different countries
and posters of well-known heroes
from around the world like Dr Martin
Luther King Jr. and Amelia Earhart.

"My family is from everywhere,"
said Avina, laughing. "Sometimes
I can't remember all the places! I
brought apple pie because my dad
grew up on an apple farm, so that's
our tradition!"

"I am not sure where my family

is from," added Jessica. "But it must be a *huggy* country because my grandma likes to hug me all the time!"

"Mine too!" Avina agreed.

"Would you like to try a cookie, Sadiq?" asked Owen. "My mum made them from a secret family recipe. She found it on the back of the chocolate chips bag!"

"That's a great tradition, Owen!" said Sadiq. He helped himself to an extra-gooey cookie. He was glad to see his friend happy.

"The festival is starting soon," said Sadiq. "I have to get back to my stall before Zaza eats all the halwa!"

Owen laughed and waved.

Sadiq took off running. The festival was turning out even better than he'd imagined.

GLOSSARY

advisor someone who leads or gives advice

beta term of affection for a young boy in the Hindi language

compliment tell someone they have done something well

compost waste materials that will naturally decay

convince persuade or talk someone into something

cowrie sea animal; its shell is thick and humped, and is often speckled and glossy

exhibition centre large building where events are held for many people to attend

hijab hair covering traditionally worn by Muslim women

Horn of Africa easternmost part of Africa, including Somalia, Ethiopia and sometimes other countries

laddu sweet treat shaped like a ball

multicultural combining or including different cultures

nani grandmother in Hindi

pachisi ancient board game from India

recipe list of ingredients and instructions to cook or bake something

soapstone somewhat soft rock that is often grey, green, brown or blue

unique unusual, or one of a kind

TALK ABOUT IT

1. Sadiq wants his school to have a multicultural festival after visiting one with his classmates. Have you ever researched your family's culture? Did you learn anything you didn't already know?

2. Sadiq's family brings food for the festival. Does your family have any cultural foods? What are they called? Have you shared them with your friends?

3. Owen struggles to identify his culture for the multicultural festival. Think about your own family. Can you relate to Owen? Can you guess what Owen might be feeling?

WRITE IT DOWN

1. Does your school have a multicultural festival? If not, write a letter to your teacher or headteacher about why you should have one. Who would do the planning? How many students would need to volunteer?

2. All cultures are fascinating. Research yours by asking a parent or grandparent, or by going to the library. Write down all of the facts you learn and share them with your friends or siblings.

3. If you could visit any country or city, where would you go? Make a list of the reasons you'd like to go there.

MAKE YOUR OWN MULTICULTURAL FESTIVAL!

Sadiq can't wait for the multicultural festival. How about you? With the help of an adult, make your own festival stall and invite your friends and siblings for extra fun!

WHAT YOU NEED:

- Cardboard box or flat surface
- Poster
- Felt-tip pens or marker pens
- Cultural foods, clothing, flags, games, art and more!

WHAT YOU DO:

1. Use the cardboard box or flat surface as your cultural stall.

2. Write the name of your culture or the country your family is from on the poster. Hang it proudly in front of or above your stall.

3. Tell your family and friends about your culture and encourage them to learn more!

4. If your family has more than one culture, make more stalls or combine different cultures into one stall!

CREATORS

Siman Nuurali grew up in Kenya. She now lives in the United States. Siman and her family are Somali – just like Sadiq and his family! She and her five children love to play badminton and board games together. Siman works at a Children's Hospital, and in her spare time she enjoys writing and reading.

Christos Skaltsas was born and raised in Athens, Greece. For the past fifteen years, he has worked as a freelance illustrator for children's book publishers. In his free time, he loves playing with his son, collecting vinyl records and travelling around the world.